The After

PALMETTO
PUBLISHING
Charleston, SC
www.PalmettoPublishing.com

Hardcover ISBN: 9798822963122
Paperback ISBN: 9798822961753
eBook ISBN: 9798822961760

The After

THE STORY OF ONE PIG'S JOURNEY
FINDING HIS FOREVER HOME

A NOVEL BY

Julie Cerros

This book is dedicated to those who confront uncomfortable truths and challenge societal norms. In the words of William Wilberforce, "You may choose to look the other way, but you can never say again that you didn't know."

The reason I dedicate myself to helping animals so much is because there are already so many people dedicated to hurting them.

—Erik Daniel Shein

The
Journey

He awoke to a frigid day. It was the end of fall or maybe winter already. The ground was frozen, and the trailer the man left him to live in was too cold to lean against or rest inside. He almost preferred this to the heat, although both burned his dry skin.

He moved in the small pile of straw they had left him and felt the cold metal underneath. He knew it wouldn't get warmer sitting there, so he decided to get up and see if there would be sun today. As he arose, he felt his brother, Batty, stir next to him.

Batty was a little younger than he was but bigger and for sure gentler. For this reason, the humans didn't get as mad at him and would sometimes give him bananas. Batty had learned to be quiet and take the hits when they came. Sometimes this didn't work in his favor, and because he didn't fight back, the big man would get mad and hit him more, but he could take it. People largely left him alone unless they were moving the two of them again. This last time was better than "The Before." In "The

Before," they were in hot and humid conditions with lots of land around and hundreds of pigs in the distance. He and Batty weren't allowed out of their small area, but they could occasionally see the pigs being moved from barn to barn by the man. Sometimes they could see the sun go down.

He thought the worst was that they feared him because of how quickly he had grown. To get him to move, they would poke him with sharp instruments that cut his skin or blast him with hard water that hurt. They could have just asked him to move, but they didn't talk to him.

It had been a long time since he or Batty had had a gentle touch or a kind look. He remembered the first summer when he was small. The humans back then were friendly and loved having him around. He had a soft bed by the hearth inside, and he remembered treats and snout kisses. It seemed the humans got scared after that summer, and he was forced to live outside and alone. Batty had arrived before fall, and that was three summers ago. They were moved shortly after that. He couldn't remember receiving kindness since.

He was awake now. He nosed Batty to get up and stepped down from the tiny trailer into the snow. He walked over to the bowls and found them empty. He thought it had been a few days since they had seen any humans. The old one who looked out the window at them in the day had been taken away in a rush of light and sound a few days ago, and there had been no one at the house since. Batty stepped down out of the trailer. His long body seemed to take the entire length of it, but he was glad that his brother was big. It helped when they had to huddle together during the cold nights to keep from freezing. However, it did not help during the summers, and Batty slept alone during the hot nights.

In "The Before," Batty had become friends with a barn mouse who would eat the grains that fell from his bowl. He would spend nights outside with his friend, Penny, tucked into his shoulder. They were the best of friends until the man who tossed them grains over the fence brought Penny some blue-looking food, and she got horribly sick and died a few days later. Batty slept alone after that.

Batty stood next to him at the bowls and looked down. "No food today?" he asked.

He replied, "Looks that way. Let's see if we can get some water off the boards." They walked over to a pile of old boards where the dew collected and the snow melted first. Sometimes, they were lucky and got water to drink. Not today. At least not this early. It was too cold, and the sun was not peeking out yet. They would have to wait. They walked back to nap outside the trailer.

What seemed like hours later, they awoke to the sound of a car driving along the gravel road. Food! They struggled to stand up and looked over at the car. He hadn't seen this one before, and it was headed to the house. He watched as three people got out and went inside. He looked to the windows and saw them go from room to room, finally stopping in front of the window where the old lady had sat and watched them each day. They stood there and pointed and talked and pointed at them some more. They were not smiling. They left the house, got in the car, and drove away.

"No food," said Batty.

"No, but we should be able to get water from the snow now. Let's try."

It was getting dark and cold. He and Batty had been lying in the little sun that had come out and had been able to get water from the puddles. They turned to go to the trailer before darkness fell. Batty had difficulty stepping up with his bad leg, and it was harder to get up in there in the dark. They heard a car. They turned and saw a familiar green car drive up to the trailer. It was the woman who sometimes brought them food. She got out of the car with food and a jug of water! She ran up to the bowls, saying she was very sorry, but there was so much work with the little ones, and there was no time to come all the way out here. She was here now, and what did they want from her anyway? She was only one person. Bowls full, she ran to the car and drove off.

He and Batty rushed over to the bowls. While he grunted and yelled to get more, he made sure that Batty got to take in more food than he did. They were both starving slowly, but Batty needed more, and he needed Batty to be okay. He took his time licking the empty bowl while Batty drank his fill of fresh water. He then went to the water bowl and pushed fresh snow into the left-over water. He knew it would melt faster when the sun hit it in the morning, and his bones felt more snow coming. Knowing they might not see food or water again for a while, he thought he had better prepare. He followed Batty into the trailer and lay down next to him.

The next day, it was snowing hard, and he tried to bury himself and Batty under the light straw. Even though the trailer didn't have a top and it was snowing, he knew that they could keep from freezing if they stayed together under the straw. If only his legs didn't hurt so much when it was bitter out. He worked frantically to throw straw over Batty and get under it. If the snow covered them, then there would be some insulation. They could keep warm if it stayed cold and the snow stayed frozen. If it rained and they got wet, then all bets were off. Batty had almost died last month during the first cold snap of the season. Batty had turned blue that terrifying night, and he had felt Batty's heart racing so fast he thought it would jump out of his chest as he lay there next to him, trying to keep him warm. He hadn't believed Batty would make it through that night, and he knew he wouldn't make it without Batty. He thought of that night as he worked frantically to keep Batty's temperature from dropping.

It was after dark when he heard a loud truck approaching. The lights hit the trailer just as it began to rain. The food woman got out and ran to the front of the trailer, banging on the metal and waking up Batty. She sprinted back and forth as a small car drove up. Another woman got out in the rain and watched as the food woman drove the truck around and hooked up the trailer. The food woman then came around the back and shut the door. He heard the lock rattle into place. It was pouring rain now; the frozen snow on their coats melted as the rain pelted them, and the straw was getting wet. He started to panic. Batty would be soaked through soon and start losing heat! She still had not said one word to them as she looked through the rusted metal and walked back to the front.

They were moving! The trailer was being pulled, and for the next two hours, they rode in the freezing rain, pelted by hard drops along the freeway. Batty was getting cold and had already been carsick. It was all he could do to hover over his brother and try to keep some of the rain off him. He wanted to give him warmth and hoped it would stop soon.

He was losing hope when he felt the trailer slow. They turned off the freeway onto a small road. It was still raining hard, and now it was mixed with snow. It felt like they were higher now. It was much colder, and he couldn't feel his hooves touching the cold metal. Batty was shaking, buried in the wet straw. They turned down a dirt road and saw lights ahead.

He wondered if they were being taken to be slaughtered. He tried not to think about things like that and never talked to Batty about it. He knew of the places and had heard the other pig's cries at the last site where they were. He had listened to their anguish and had seen the tears as the others were pulled and pushed into the big trucks to be driven off. He didn't know what the places looked like from the outside, as so few had escaped, and he thought the escape tales of those who fought to be free and live happily ever after seemed like stories you told the young ones to give them hope. He turned his attention to the lights again and hoped he wouldn't see one of the big, windowless buildings he'd pictured when listening to escape tales he had heard over the years.

The truck stopped. Humans with lights were walking in what was now hail. He couldn't see faces or hear voices over the hard pummeling of the icy pellets on the metal sides of the trailer. The hail was coming down sideways and hitting the rusted-out panels on the locked doors, which were now creaking open. He could see the ground through the hail and moving lights. He saw the food woman at the door and now he heard her yell at them to get out of the trailer. He hesitated, unsure how far it was to the ground. He heard her say Batty was "easier" and saw a rake shoved through the side to prod the sick boy. Batty saw it coming and tried getting up quickly to avoid the pain. Batty stumbled out onto the wet dirt and hail and followed the lights.

He was left alone in the open trailer and rushed after Batty, jumping into the unknown. He hit the ground and slipped but quickly got his footing, and his little legs ran down the path after the lights. He saw Batty enter a fenced area and then a tiny straw-filled shed. A gate behind them closed. He heard a woman say, "Are you sure they are all right?" as the group walked off. Exhausted and unsure, he and Batty moved into the warm straw, lay down, and closed their eyes. There was nothing more they could do. He had learned long ago he had no control over his fate.

The following day, he awoke, unsure of where he was. Batty was asleep next to him, and he was warm and dry. He let himself lie there, his mind racing, wondering if he should get up or wait to see what the day brought. Then he remembered "The Before" and quickly struggled to stand, not wanting to be surprised again. He slowly looked around. There was warmth on his back, and he glanced up. There were red lights above their heads that were giving warmth to the straw. No wonder Batty was sleeping so soundly. They hadn't been warm since summer. The lights felt good on his sore legs, and he was reluctant to leave their little building, but he heard a noise and slowly went toward the door. He poked his snout out of the door. He saw snow and trees but not much else.

He took a step out and peered around the side. Someone was coming! He saw someone carrying a bucket across a field, and behind them, he saw another figure struggling through the snow. They were covered head to toe in thick, puffy coats and oversized hats pulled so low he couldn't see faces. Their tall boots crunched across the ground as they came closer. He'd better get Batty up now. He stuck his head back inside and nosed Batty's legs. "Hey, get up! Someone is coming."

Batty grunted and sat up, shaking the sleep from his mind. They were both quiet and suddenly terrified.

The people came closer. The two pigs heard the gate open and saw heads poke around the corner of the door. Two sets of eyes landed on them and suddenly widened in surprise at the same time.

"Well, hello, handsome boys," said one muffled voice.

"Oh gosh, they are so big," said the other.

Both sentences came out simultaneously, and it took him a minute to decipher what they said. He realized neither voice was harsh or unpleasant sounding. The one closest to the door took off their face coverings and bent down.

"I bet you're starving. Let's get you some food."

He wasn't sure what was happening, but he was hungry and didn't see any pipes or sticks in their hands. His stomach won, and he nodded to Batty that they should follow the humans. He came forward and stood in front of Batty in case things went wrong. The faces disappeared as they smelled food! He looked around the corner and heard a woman saying, "Okay, boys, come eat."

He and Batty looked at each other, and their stomachs growled at the same time. They slowly moved toward the smell. They shuffled through the snow in front of the door and turned the corner, hesitating as they walked over to the gate. The people had steaming bowls of warm food, which they placed through the openings. He and Batty could no longer stop themselves. They dug into the food. He couldn't remember a time when they had both had an entire bowl of food, and it hadn't been warmed up for him since he was little. He made sure Batty was eating and inhaled his bowl, no longer caring what was coming at that moment. Real hunger overcame his flight response.

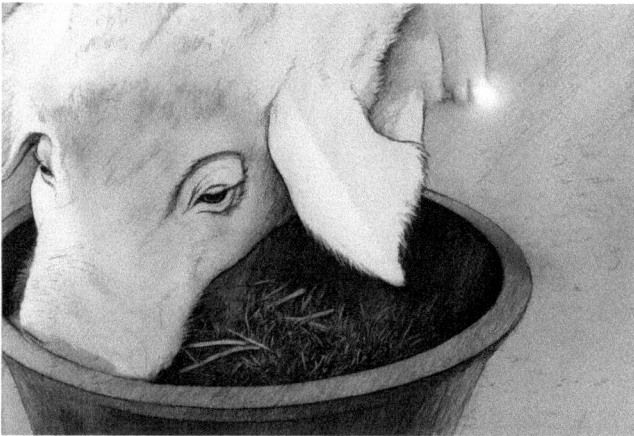

A full two minutes later, the bowls were empty and licked clean. They slowly came back to their surroundings. He thought he could handle what came next easier without the gnawing hunger that was always in his belly. The people came over. He shrank back. He saw a hand reaching for him. He instinctively pulled his head back and ducked. He heard the female gasp and say, "Oh, they've been beaten."

He thought, *You have no idea.*

The man said, "Okay, boy, let's take it nice and slow and get you some water."

He saw the man bring in a huge trough and a hose and heard the water start flowing into the trough. He suddenly got very thirsty but was afraid it was a trick. He hung back and didn't let Batty advance to the water. He remembered when they used to hold his head under the water, and he would never be that close to water with humans around again.

The man finished filling the trough, pulled up the hose, and went out the gate. The humans stood outside the gate, watching them, talking softly while cleaning the bowls he and Batty had eaten out of. He slowly approached the trough and put his mouth to the cool water. It was clean and fresh, and he found he could not stop drinking. He drank his fill for the first time in months, maybe longer. Then he raised his head and called Batty over to drink.

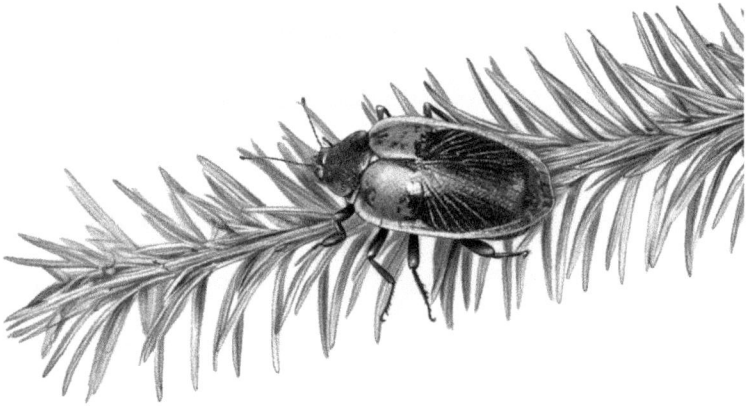

After drinking, they weren't sure what to do. Should they go back into the little shed with straw or walk around? He waited to be yelled at, but the man just said, "Okay, boys, you settle in, and we'll check on you in a bit." Then he left! What to do? He and Batty just looked at each other and slowly gazed around. They took in the area they had been brought to last night for the first time.

As he looked, he realized they were alone, and he thought it might be okay to walk around a bit. He would keep the shed in sight; they could run back at any time if they heard someone. All they heard now were birds and a dog barking in the distance. He and Batty slowly moved away from the trough and started toward the fence line. He made his way carefully past the trees. He had seen trees in the far distance but had never been allowed next to one before. They smelled amazing! He nudged one with his snout, and a bug fell right off the branch it had been lounging on and onto the ground. Batty jumped behind him, and he let out a laugh. He realized it felt like he hadn't laughed in a very long time.

With Batty behind him, he moved forward while keeping the shed in sight. He finally reached the fence. He could see through it and saw some machines across the field but no animals or humans. He let Batty pass next to him while they looked on and stood in the sunlight.

After a few minutes, thinking that was long enough to be so far from safety, he turned to go back to the shed. He told Batty he was very brave, and although he did not know this and wasn't sure of anything, he told him he thought they would be fine and he had a very good feeling about this place. He watched as some of the worry in Batty's face lessened, and that was worth the lie.

They settled into the straw in the shed with their backs to the far wall. He knew how to prepare them for surprise visits by humans. He hadn't seen the iron pipes or pitchforks yet, but they didn't always come out right after they arrived in a new place—except in "The Before." He tried not to think of that too much.

One time they were moved, and it seemed like the humans were going to be kind, but the man would come in the evenings and poke and scratch them with the forks just for fun while the woman was inside and couldn't hear their cries. He thought it best to prepare for the worst. At least here, he didn't hear the pain of other pigs when they went inside the buildings. He only heard birds now and saw the snow start to fall. He felt himself drift off in the warm straw to the sound of the birdsong.

He fell into a deep sleep and started to dream. He hadn't dreamed in what felt like years. After all, he needed to stay vigilant and sharp to protect them! He never fully rested. Now he slept and dreamed of fresh water, mudholes, and the little girl he knew long ago. He heard her laugh and saw her coming through the door of the home he once lived in. If he sat when she told him to, she let him jump onto the bed and fall asleep next to her. He would feel her heart slowing and her breathing deepen as she fell quiet. He could snuggle closer to her and felt safe and loved. He didn't like to think about the next times, and he kicked out in his dream as he drifted deeper into thinking about the man. He had known to stay away from him and out of reach of his boots when the girl was gone in the day. He had taken great care to make himself small and unnoticeable so he didn't receive any attention.

There was a place under the porch where he could crawl and be quiet, and, mostly, no one would see him or remember he was around. If the adults were mad and yelling that day, he would back all the way under so his nose didn't stick out and he couldn't be seen from the steps. At first, he was very scared of the dark and kept his eyes shut very tight. After a few times doing this, he opened his eyes and found six eyes staring back at him! He whipped his head back and forth, trying to make sense of what he was seeing and realized he was lying in a raccoon den. He shut his eyes tight again and tried to slow his breathing. He didn't hear anything.

He slowly opened one eye. Three fluffy raccoons were looking at him. Whap! He shut his eye. He stayed that way and thought maybe they would go away. He peeked. Nope. They were still looking over at him—not angrily or cruelly, just curiously and maybe kindly?

He shut his eyes and said, "Go away please."

He heard a giggle. He opened one eye. He saw the smallest, fluffiest one was giggling, and he noticed they were very young. He opened the other eye. Now he said more loudly, "Go away!"

All three started giggling, and he saw the kind faces behind the laughter.

The largest one said, "Hi there. You're in our home. Would you like some apples? We've just brought them back from the tree across the field."

He gulped and said he would. The little one ran to a box that was in the corner and returned with an apple.

He took it gently and said, "Thank you."

The middle one said quietly, "We know you need to hide from the man. You are welcome here anytime, and you don't have to keep your eyes shut. We're all just trying to help each other. Tuff, the new puppy, comes down here when the man gets mad or the woman forgets to feed him. We take care of each other." He saw her kind smile and was grateful to feel safe.

Someone was calling him out of his dream, and he heard Batty in his ear saying, "Something is happening— Wake up!"

He struggled out of his dream and onto his feet. They cautiously peeked outside the door where they'd heard the commotion. Now there were four humans standing in the snow! One was so tall and big he thought he must be a giant. The other new one was very short and skinny, and they were talking with the two who had fed them that morning. They were looking and pointing in the direction of the machines in the distance and then back at him and Batty again. The woman looked worried, and he heard something about lights and cold and snow.

The giant laughed gently, and as he turned to them, he heard him say, "They'll be fine; it's not that cold, and they have thick coats from living outside. We'll string up more lamps to keep them extra warm and a camera for you to keep an eye on them while we put up their barn. When is Jack coming out to see them?"

The woman responded, but she was looking in the direction of the machines, and he couldn't hear what she said. He wondered who Jack was, but he didn't want to worry Batty, so he kept quiet as they watched them walk away to a clearing over by the machines.

He and Batty took this time to go to the trough and get more water. The constant feeling of thirst was lessening, and Batty said his headache was going away. He suggested they lie down in the shed and play a game they sometimes used to pass the time. It was called "I Spy." His raccoon family taught it to him. Boy, did they have new things to spy! He started with "I spy something green…" They did this back and forth for the next little while until Batty fell asleep, and he could relax knowing that for now they were okay.

A little while later, he heard the first man and woman come back to the shed, and they had more food—this time, they brought fruit. Food twice in one day, and he hadn't had fruit since his visits under the porch. He nudged Batty awake, and they slowly walked toward the fence. The woman put bowls with cut-up fruit in front of each of them and told them to eat while she mixed their food. They sniffed and started to sample the fresh fruit. He could taste banana and apples and some kind of berries. It didn't matter; he was already drooling while he dug in, and Batty did the same. They were just finishing their snack when the man put two bowls of warm food down and told them to eat up. He said Jack was coming tomorrow to see them.

He again wondered who Jack was, but he had a full belly, and it didn't worry him as much as it had earlier. He and Batty crawled under the straw and fell fast asleep.

He felt Batty move next to him and realized he had slept through the night. He tried to remember the last time he had slept that long and finally gave up. He opened his eyes and looked out. A truck was in the dirt by the machines. He hadn't even heard it drive up, and he worried he might be getting too comfortable when he wasn't even sure they were safe. Batty was fully awake now and stared cautiously at the truck.

"What's that?" he asked.

He replied he wasn't sure yet, and they crawled a bit closer to the door to see. The man and woman were there with a cowboy and a couple of kids. They had seen many cowboys in "The Before" and knew to be cautious and stay away. They were all getting out of the truck and putting things in their pockets. He and Batty watched the people close the doors, and they all walked over to the gate by the shed. The cowboy didn't bother with the gate but easily jumped over the fence in one motion. The kids opened the gate, and all three walked over and stood in front of them. He and Batty stood up quickly and backed into the corner inside the shed. He stood protectively in front of his brother. He felt Batty tremble and start to cry.

The cowboy spoke. "Hi, boys, let's get a look at you. I'm not going to hurt you."

He looked into the cowboy's face and realized he looked kind. His voice was soft as he asked, "Can I see you?"

He tentatively took one step forward, still protecting Batty. He knew what happened when he refused a human's ask. The cowboy turned to the kids and said that they had time and it would be better to give them space. He told the kids they should all go look at the new barn and see if they would be more comfortable walking out of the shed without so many people there. The man came around the corner and said, "Sounds good, Jack," and they all walked through the gate and across the field.

So that was Jack, he thought. He let Batty out of the corner and saw he had stopped crying and now looked a little curious. They both inched forward and came out of the shed to peer across the field. All the humans were over by the machines, but he didn't see Jack anywhere. Suddenly he felt a pinch on his back, and just as the world went sideways, he realized Jack was standing next to him and Batty was sleeping on the ground. He had no time to understand what was going on before he was asleep.

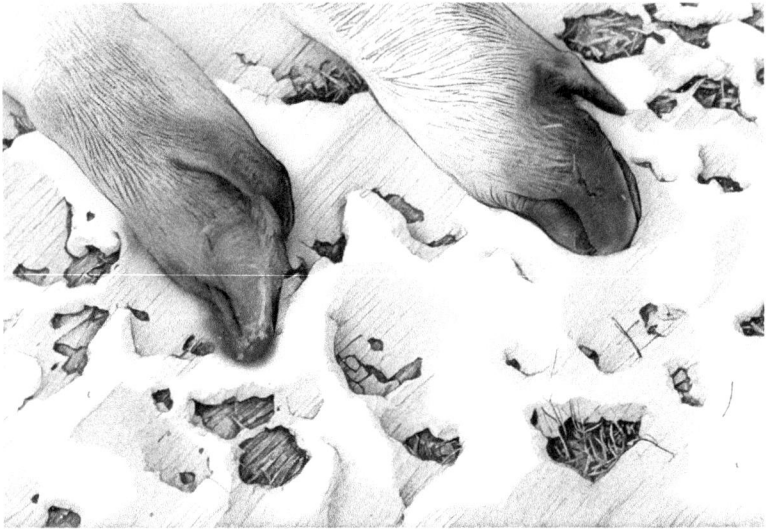

His mouth was dry, and he was hungry. He was out-side but had no idea if it was night or day and had a hard time opening his eyes. He finally pried them open and realized he was on the ground by the fence, and a blanket was covering him. It was getting dark! He felt that was weird but couldn't remember how he got there, why he was on the ground, or why Batty was next to him, also with a blanket covering him. He turned his head and struggled to sit up when he saw the two humans sitting next to him!

Oooof! His head hurt. He shook his head and tried to make sense of what was happening. The woman looked worried and asked him if he was thirsty. He suddenly realized he was very thirsty and wobbled to his feet. She told him to stay there. She ran to get a bowl with water and brought it to him. He leaned down and drank until the bowl was empty. He was trying to recall the last thing he remembered when he saw Batty open his eyes. The woman ran to refill the water for Batty. He also drank until it was empty.

Batty started to say something to him and then stopped. His tongue came out of his mouth and moved across his snout, and he pulled it back into his mouth quickly. In and out, in and out, it went a few more times. He smiled wide. Batty looked at him and opened his mouth so he could see in. For the last year, Batty's bottom right tusk had been growing into his gums and back up again, cutting into the roof of his mouth. He'd had a hard time eating and had been complaining of headaches. Now it was short, and the left one was the same size! Neither of the bottom tusks were cutting into his gums, and although the gums were red and looked swollen, all his teeth now fit in his mouth.

The man asked how his mouth felt and then said, "Wait until you see your feet!"

They both looked down. They saw their feet. The nails were short and no longer growing over each other and underneath their feet. Batty stood up, wobbling, and took a small step. He found he now had footing on solid ground. He took another cautious step and discovered he could walk without pain. He stepped faster now, spun in a circle, and suddenly took off running across the pasture.

He watched his brother run for the first time in years and smiled. He felt an emotion he wasn't familiar with and thought it must be hope.

The next morning after breakfast (again!), they heard the machines across the way start up. After each of them had a long drink, wondering how they'd lived without fresh water for so long, they made their way through the trees and peeked over the fence. They saw the men from the other day putting up a side of a building. The giant was on a machine and moving dirt back and forth while the little one ran back and forth with poles and looked very busy. They watched for a bit and then went to nap under the trees.

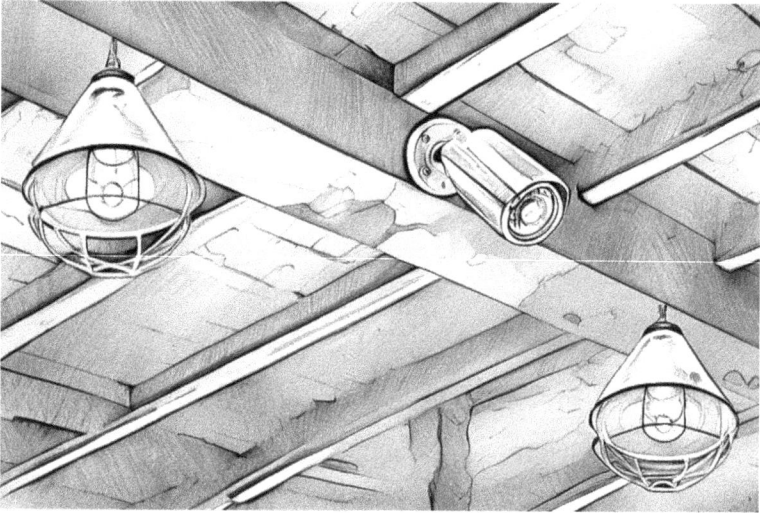

It was afternoon when they awoke and realized light snow was coming down. They moved toward the shelter and noticed it was lit up all red inside! They poked their snouts in and saw three more big red bulbs hanging from the ceiling and a black box in the corner. They felt the warmth radiating to where they were standing and decided it was better inside than where they were standing since the snow was coming down harder with big flakes now. They stepped into the warmth and settled into the dry straw. A short time later, the woman came by and poked her head in.

"Hi, boys, looks like you found the extra heat lamps and camera. Now I can see how you are from home. Y'all hungry?"

Having been asked that, they realized they were, and he could hear Batty's stomach grumble. The thought crossed his mind that he'd better not get used to this regular food because it could turn into "The Before," but he didn't like to think about that and nudged Batty toward the door.

She told them not to get up, and from behind her appeared two warm bowls of food. As she set one each before them in bed, she said, "You boys can eat here inside since it's snowing hard now and I don't want you getting wet. Josh says your new barn will be ready in two weeks." Her head disappeared again and then showed right up with a fresh bowl of water she put in between them, telling them to stay inside where it was warm and dry until this storm passed.

Well okay then, he thought. *I might as well settle back down for dinner and a little nap.* They ate in the warmth, drank a bit, and went straight back to lying in the comfortable straw piles. He looked up, through the door, and could see the snow falling. He was thankful it was not falling on them and he didn't need to worry about Batty tonight. He drifted off, warm and content, with his brother snoring away next to him.

The next days were spent largely inside while the storm raged outside. They were grateful for everything they were experiencing. They had spent the past few years with little to no shelter and trading off being cold and wet for being hot and sunburned, depending on the season. The woman kept bringing them food and water twice a day.

The storm passed after four days, and they spent the following two weeks settling into a routine of sleeping, eating, exploring the little pasture, and watching the giant man and little one from afar. The two men moved quickly and laughed throughout each day, yelling back and forth over the machines. They even came to talk to him and Batty each day while they ate lunch. They would put pieces of fruit and greens through the fence, and after they went back to work, he would go retrieve them for him and Batty. He thought, *They must know we're eating these*, since he'd caught the little one looking out of the corner of his eye and smiling as he retrieved them one day.

One afternoon, they wandered over to the fence to see the work and realized there was a barn standing there. It had fencing and bales and bales of hay stacked in front of it. He suddenly got nervous. He remembered "The Before" and the giant barns and the screams. He told Batty to go back to the shelter, and they went to one corner together and lay down. Batty was trembling, and there wasn't much to say to reassure him so he kept quiet and his guard up.

A little later in the evening, he heard the woman call for them. She said she wanted to show them their new area. He felt the tears stream down his face. Batty had his eyes shut tight, and he could feel him shaking uncontrollably.

"Boys!" She poked her head in and saw them. The smile on her face faded as soon as she saw their expressions and the tears. "Oh my gosh, what is wrong? What is it? Honey, get in here!"

The man stuck his head in as he said, "Hey, aren't you moving them?"

She said she was but asked him to look at them and see if they were hurt. "They won't move, and he's crying." She reached toward Batty, and he pushed his brother down and forced them both back farther into the corner. He shielded Batty as his fear notched up even more. He closed his eyes and waited for the pain to come.

In "The Before," when the man wanted them to move, he never asked. He took the tool he used to break apart the straw and poked them with it. The first jab was the worst, as it almost always punctured their skin with each of the prongs and made them bleed profusely. They would move as quickly as they could get up and go, but if they were asleep or didn't know which way he wanted them to go, it sometimes took a while. Then they would be left with gashes and punctures that would get infected in the filth they were made to lie in if they didn't take care. The raccoons showed them ways to clean the wounds and keep them covered. They learned about the different plants around the area they could put on them that would make them feel better, but he hadn't been looking for that here. He had let his guard down.

He braced for impact. He didn't feel anything. He slowly opened one eye. She was sitting in front of them quietly, looking at them with what he thought was care or concern maybe. She said slowly, "Boys, your new barn is ready for you, but if you aren't ready for it, we can wait." She looked up at the man and said maybe he could bring some treats. The man ducked out of sight and quickly reappeared with his hands full of peanuts.

He opened both eyes now and felt Batty's nose come out from under him.

She took some nuts from the man's hands and slowly offered one to him. He moved his mouth closer to her hand and stuck out his tongue. She placed one on his tongue, and he sucked it up and crunched on it. Batty's head was now completely out from under him, and he stuck his tongue out. The man laughed and startled Batty, and his tongue went quickly back into his mouth. The man reached out and put one in front of Batty's snout, and it quickly disappeared with a loud slurp.

He moved a bit and looked past the two humans. He didn't see any tools around. He signaled to Batty to stand up, and they both rolled over and stood. The woman also stood up, dusted herself off slowly, not making any sudden moves, and walked to the door.

She said, "Let's all walk to the new barn with some treats, shall we?"

She held out her hand with some peanuts in it, and he went slowly over and opened his mouth. She put one in, and he crunched. Batty was suddenly next to him with his tongue out, and the man put one on it as they stepped into the walkway between the fences. The four of them walked slowly across the field with peanuts appearing on the ground every couple of feet. He and Batty had their heads down, sniffing and sucking up the crunchy treats as soon as they appeared.

He sensed the halting of the group and looked up. They were all standing in front of the barn they had seen from across the field. Fear gripped him again, but he realized this felt different. There were no screams, and he didn't smell blood. This big barn was well lit, with lots of hay and dirt, not concrete. He took a step forward to stand next to the woman, and she leaned down and asked him if he liked his new barn. He looked over at Batty and stepped forward.

The woman opened a gate and walked into another area with a huge water trough. She clicked the gate so it stayed open, and he and Batty followed her in. She continued forward, through some wooden doors into the barn. They could see past her into a well-lit barn with hay stacked in the middle up to the second story. She walked slowly, glancing back to make sure they were following. She stopped in front of some big metal bins and opened one. The smell of peanuts urged them forward, and she held out some in her hand. Batty's tongue shot past his head and snatched all that were there. The loud crunching sound of his chewing echoed in the barn. She laughed, and that also echoed off the walls.

He felt a calm come over him as he looked around. It was quiet and peaceful, warm and dry. He inched forward to the fresh water he saw flowing in the trough that ran from the inside to the outside water tubs they had passed. He put his snout in the water and drank quickly. It was fresh and cool. He slowed his drinking and took in mouthfuls. He felt Batty next to him starting to drink, and he took a step back and looked up at the man. He was fluffing straw in the stalls next to him. The man stepped back and told the woman that would be good for their first night in their new barn. Suddenly two apples appeared from the woman's pockets. She laid one apple in each pile of straw and stepped out of the stall.

"Welcome home, boys."

He was suddenly exhausted and the straw looked so comfortable. He walked in and went to the right-side pile. He nodded to Batty and gestured his snout toward the left side. Batty stepped in and nosed the straw. They watched as Batty took a mouthful and started rearranging his bed. The more his brother dug in, the happier he got.

He tunneled and pushed some toward the right side. He spied the apple in his pile, picked it up, and belly-flopped right in the middle of the straw. He then looked up at the humans in the doorway. He crushed the apple with his strong jaws and slurped happily while juice ran down his chin. He could feel the joy of the moment radiating from his brother and a wide smile slowly spread across his face.

The humans looked at them both warmly and said good night. They left, saying they would be back in the morning. He nosed his apple toward Batty, who happily slurped it up. He felt warm and settled down in the soft straw. He couldn't keep his eyes open any longer, and he dropped off to sleep.

He felt sun on his face and slowly opened his eyes. He remembered where he was and looked to his left. All he could see was Batty's nose. His brother had completely buried himself under the straw and was snoring loudly. Realizing it had been a very long time since he had seen Batty sleep so deeply, he didn't disturb him but stood up slowly and went to the stall door. He looked both ways but didn't see anyone. The sun was just rising and beginning to peek over the mountains he saw in the distance. It was starting to flood the barn with warm light. He stretched his legs and realized they weren't stiff today. He walked to the outside troughs. He still didn't see any humans, but there was a frog swimming in the trough. He didn't disturb him and went to the other side to take a cool drink. It was peaceful, and the only sounds were birds and Batty's snoring coming from the main barn. Since Batty was still asleep and safe and he didn't see anything to be fearful about, he thought he would explore for a short bit.

He eased slowly toward an open gate that looked like it led to a pasture that had tall trees across the way. He was cautious but eager to see the trees. "The Before" had no trees, and he had spent all his time in a building, never seeing the sun or moon or feeling the ground. During that time, he only knew hard concrete and metal and the three-by-three cage he was kept in. When he was there, the memory of outside with the little girl had faded, and his world went to gray.

The last couple years had been better, and even with the lack of real shelter and the brutal seasons, he'd appreciated being outside rather than caged, but never in his life had he seen trees like these. The raccoons had spoken of living in them, and he would ask them to repeat their stories and adventures in the wild over and over until he felt he was actually there. He thought these must be the trees they had spoken about. He had dreamed of their majesty up close and was excited to smell them for himself. He never imagined he would get to experience this. There were many times when he thought he would not make it out of "The Before."

He walked through the gates and toward the tallest tree he could see on the other side of the pasture. Moving slowly and quietly so he could hear Batty's snoring, he felt the ground crunch beneath his feet as the sun rose. He wanted to feel everything he could, as he knew how quickly everything could change. He noticed the dew on the small bushes and the smell of berries as he walked. He watched a large group of crows talking in the towering tree he was walking toward. They all turned to watch him as he moved closer. He stopped and listened for Batty. He heard a particularly loud snore and started walking again. He smelled something that he knew from the raccoon's description must be actual pine! The smell was stronger now, and he was so happy! He could finally smell it for himself. He realized he was crying. With tears streaming down his face, he walked up to the tall tree and looked up. It was so tall he had to sit down to look up and see the top. It was the most majestic thing he'd ever seen. "Hey!" he heard in his ear. Startled, he fell over and looked up.

A crow was standing over him with a grin on his face. "Whoops, sorry I startled you. I'm Ralph."

He rolled over and sat up. "Hi."

The crow called Ralph said, "We've been watching you and your brother. Glad you guys are here! We've seen the humans getting the land clear for a while now, and the big fence went up last week. Looks like you guys are here at the right time."

He stood all the way up now and looked across the field at the big fence. "Oh, we haven't really seen a lot of the place, just the shed we were in and now the barn."

Ralph hopped on over to him. "That barn's a nice one! We fly this whole mountain, and that is one good barn. Water, heat, air, fans, the works. You boys are gonna love it. Good thing the outside gates and fence are up, though, or you'd have to deal with Freddie coming and stealing your food." He chuckled and hopped around, delighted. "She's the neighborhood alpaca who comes by every day. The female human—she's called CJ by the way—gives her apples but has been trying to keep her at the fence line since she likes to come up to the house and chase the dogs. Freddie thinks it's hilarious. When they moved to this land in spring, there was only high grass and the house. They've cleared the land, put up some buildings, and run water across it. The fence and gates and barn must be for you boys. CJ has been out here talking about how excited she is to bring new residents here. This is her favorite spot to sit and rest here under this tree you were smelling. Where'd you come from?"

He looked at Ralph and started to answer when a tear rolled down his face.

Ralph saw it and said, "Look, don't worry; we will have lots of time to talk. Hey, isn't that your brother?"

He suddenly realized he hadn't been listening for the snoring and turned quickly to see Batty walking across the field with a sleepy look on his face. Suddenly, he heard a loud squawking from the tree, and several crows left the branches and flew toward the nearest pasture.

"Whoops," said Ralph, "the young ones are hungry, and I'd better get to them before they start bothering the hawks. They'll chase them all morning. Tell your brother I said hello, and we'll introduce you to the whole family real soon." He took off from the ground and rushed to catch up to the little ones, who were already specks in the sky.

He turned to Batty as he lumbered up. "Well, good morning, sleepyhead."

Batty smiled at him and looked quickly around, a flicker of fear showing in his eyes as he scanned the pasture.

He met his brother's eyes and smiled. "We have a new friend! His name is Ralph, and he and his family live in this tree. Come smell it, Batty—it's beautiful."

Batty smiled and no longer looked fearful. He straightened up, walked over to the majestic tree, and sniffed all the pine needles on the ground. He looked up and had to back up and stretch his neck to see all the way to the top as he took a big breath in and a goofy grin came over his face. He looked happy.

The next months flew by. He and Batty settled into a comfortable daily routine of regular meals and fresh water, as well as soft beds with plenty of fresh straw to lie in and alfalfa to munch on. The winter had several big storms come through, but the new barn was comfortable and warm. Ralph and his family visited often and even stayed with them when the wind was kicking up or it was very cold out. He and Batty started to slowly relax and feel more at ease with the humans, even looking forward to when they would come in to feed. He liked the smiles they gave him, and he even let the female close enough to touch his belly one day! Her touch was gentle, and he remembered the kind touch of the little girl. He continued to keep an eye out for warning signs but started to settle in. He stopped worrying so much about Batty as he saw him flourish under the regular nourishment and care they were receiving. Batty smiled now, more than he ever had, and that made him feel good.

One morning, he woke up and sensed a change in the weather. It was warmer, and he smelled fresh growth just below the surface of the pasture. He and Batty took the opportunity to lie in the sun just outside the barn and sun themselves, napping on the cool ground. He was just turning over to sun his other side when he heard a truck. He quickly rolled up onto his belly and nudged Batty out of his nap.

"Hey, get up; someone's here."

They both slowly got to their feet, shaking off the sleepy feeling as they watched a large white truck they had never seen before drive through the front gates and stop in front of the main house.

"Let's go hang out in the barn for now, okay?" he said.

Batty nodded, and they trotted back to the main barn entrance and went to their stalls. They had a good view of the truck from there. They settled down in the straw and waited to see what was going to happen next.

A woman got out of the truck and went to the house. A few minutes later, the woman and the female named CJ came out, walked to the back of the truck, and opened it. They reached in and hauled out a big carrier, careful to set it on the ground gently. They bent down and looked in. He couldn't hear what they were saying, but there seemed to be a lot of conversation, and possibly some of the talk was addressed to someone in the carrier. Now he turned his head and strained to hear the voices. He couldn't hear a thing. He saw CJ unhook the latch on the carrier and straighten up. There was a white nose poking out of the door!

Suddenly, two hooves attached to very long legs appeared and then a head with horns. He had been leaning so far out of his stall to see this that he fell over with a giant plop and startled Batty, who took one look at him with his little legs up in the air and burst out laughing. This startled the barn sparrows, who took off out of the rafters, making a ruckus and in turn causing both the women to turn and look at the barn. This gave the visitor in the crate an opportunity to jump out, hop over to the gravel hill in front of the barn, and scramble to the top, looking quite regal and very much like they were surveying their new kingdom. It was a goat!

"Well, she's out now!" said CJ. She and the other woman both stood up and walked over to the gravel hill. CJ smiled and said, "Welcome home, Mocha!"

The goat proceeded to run down the hill, straight at CJ, with her head down, in full headbutt mode!

He rolled over on his belly, just in time to see CJ step lightly to the side as the goat ran right by her. Both women laughed and started to walk back to the truck. He heard CJ say something about giving her time and space to settle in, and they turned away so he couldn't hear the rest of the conversation. Batty came and stood next to him as they watched the new arrival run in circles around the truck and back up the hill, where she lay gently down and sighed.

This new development broke up the routine he had planned for the day. He had been planning on rooting some this morning, taking a long mud bath in one of the wallows, and then moving on to a nap, but the goat's arrival changed things. He turned to Batty and said they should go hang out by the fence near the hill and see if they could get some information from Mocha. They walked over to the fence and looked at the arrival. She was lying in the sun with her eyes closed, breathing deeply.

He peered around the hill to see that both women had gone into the house and there was no one else around. He whispered, "Pssst! Hey, you on the hill!"

The goat called Mocha whipped her head around, popped up on all four legs, immediately ran down the hill toward the fence, and rammed it so hard with her horns she was flipped back on her butt and fell over with a loud thump. Batty looked shocked, and the frog that had been sunning by the wallow jumped into the water and disappeared.

"Hey, don't be afraid. We just want to say hello," he said.

Mocha slowly sat up. She looked over at them with suspicion in her eyes and glanced to the right and left at the fence, as if sensing a trap. He saw the fear in her eyes. "Honest. We just want to say hello."

Suddenly, Ralph swooped down from above and landed on the fence. "Hey, Mocha! What's up, girl?"

Mocha looked up at Ralph and smiled a huge smile as relief came over her face. She tilted her head up and nodded shyly to Ralph. "Hi, Ralph. You know where I am?"

"Yes," said Ralph, "you are at the new place in the hills Jack was talking about. Remember?"

The fear started to move out of her eyes, and she spoke to Ralph, still keeping him and Batty in her side vision in case she needed to make a quick getaway. "Oh, this is the place? He was over at Kayleigh's place doing my hooves yesterday and said I should look nice for my new home! I didn't know it was this place. He told me all about it and how there were two residents here already." Mocha's eyes darted immediately over to him and Batty before quickly looking away. "It's okay here, Ralph?" She asked the question quickly as she looked back and forth.

"Yes, Mocha. You'll be safe here."

A tear came to the corner of her eye and rolled down her cheek as he saw her entire body relax a bit.

They heard a call come from house. "Mocha, where'd you go?"

They all looked at the house as they saw CJ and the other woman come out and stand by the truck. Ralph flew off toward his tree, and Mocha trotted around the hill and looked at the women. Mocha gave one look back at him and Batty and then took off running toward CJ and the other woman with her head tilted down and her little legs galloping at full speed.

He and Batty strolled back to the barn, and Ralph fluttered down next to them in the hay. He asked Ralph to tell them more about Mocha and how he knew her. Ralph settled down in the hay and scratched his head with one foot. "Well, let's see if I can give you boys some background. She was originally from all the way out in Alabama. She and her nineteen brothers were born on a goat farm where the humans made items from the goat milk and sold them on the weekends at the markets. You boys know about how the mom goats have to stay pregnant to produce milk?" He looked up at them from the hay.

He and Batty nodded, and Batty looked a bit sad.

"Okay, so each time one of the nannies on the farm gave birth, the humans would separate the kids and keep them in a barn across the pasture. When Mocha was born, there were nineteen young bucklings already in that barn. She stayed there with them for the first few weeks until one of the little humans took a liking to her. With her being the only female that they had seen in a few years, he thought she was special and took her as his pet. She lived inside with him for a few months until he started school and quickly grew bored of her. He didn't play with her outside anymore, and she said she thought he sometimes forgot she was around. The family dog would share his food with her when the humans were out at the barns, and she still got to sleep inside by fire, but no one really spoke to her much.

"Mocha told me that she heard the woman and man talking one night and learned that the farm was not doing well. The woman had sold all of the bucklings to the butcher by then, and they were thinking of moving and not sure what to do with Mocha. The next day after she heard that, they moved her outside to the back of the property where there was a little plastic igloo of a house the dog used to be in before he got too big. They put her on a chain so she had to stay close to the little igloo and could just reach some bowls they put there, but she couldn't get out of the snow or cold completely as it was too small for her to lie in. She found a way to back in to keep the majority of the snow off her body, but her head and front legs were left outside and she would lose body heat during the storms and cold days. She said she was out there for a few weeks when one day a huge truck came in the morning, and she saw lots of activity around it well into the night. When she woke up the next morning, all was quiet. She called out to the dog, but he didn't come out his back door to visit her, and she heard no movement in the house. She couldn't go closer to see, as she was still chained up, but no one came to feed her anymore, and she ran out of water three nights later.

"Mocha doesn't know how long she was out there, but she lost energy and had given up trying to break her chain free when one afternoon she thought she heard voices. She lifted her head from the side of the igloo where she had fallen down a few days earlier and saw some humans walking across the back area toward her. She saw a kind face bend down and reach for the chain as she was picked up gently by two others. She heard a jumble of voices all together 'How long? Are you sure it's been six weeks? Yes, I saw them leave the beginning of last month; haven't seen anyone here since. She's barely holding on; we've got to get some fluids in her and get her warm. She weighs hardly anything.' She saw the chain being cut and her leg freed and doesn't remember anything after that.

"She woke up in a well-lit barn with an IV in her arm and a rabbit next to her eating some celery. She says one of the barn cats told her she was in Santa Fe, New Mexico, at a veterinary clinic. She fell back to sleep after that and then remembers waking up in a stall in a pile of warm hay. She says she was there for a few days when Kayleigh came to get her, and she's been there recuperating ever since." He looked at their faces. "You don't know who Kayleigh is, do you, boys?"

They both shook their heads.

"All right, let me get a drink, and I'll fill you in on that one too!"

Ralph hopped up and over to one of the inside troughs and sipped some water. "Nice barn, boys, nice barn!" He hopped back to the pile of hay and settled in again. "Now where was I? Kayleigh?"

They nodded.

"Kayleigh has got a sanctuary like this one down on the other side of the mountain. She's about full right now if my count is right. She has fifty-five residents, but she takes in who she can in her emergency overflow and will find them homes at other places. She took in Mocha about midwinter and has been rehabilitating her. Her back leg that was chained up has a lot of damage, and she had to do physical therapy every day. She had some frostbite from being left outside, and they've had to slowly put some weight on her since she almost starved to death. Jack—you boys know Jack—has been treating her for different issues with her hooves and horns. Her hooves looked almost as bad as yours, Batty! He and those kids he's got from the vet school are good and careful, though. They treat just about everyone here on this mountain and down the hill."

Ralph paused as something caught his attention out of the corner of his eye. He smiled a wide smile and raised his wing. "Hey, Nelson! Long time no see, buddy," he yelled over to the frog that had just jumped into the closest outside water trough. The frog named Nelson grinned and waved one of his little feet in the air as he took a big gulp of air and dove under the water. "That's Nelson; he's a good guy. He and his family are here, and he says his cousins are coming in from the lake later this summer when it gets dry down south. Okay, back to Mocha. So, Kayleigh knew CJ was building this place and had taken you boys in, so she contacted her to see if she could take in Mocha. One of my boys heard CJ making the arrangements last week, and here she is. You boys will have to show her around and make her welcome. She's a little shy at first, and her first go-to is to headbutt anyone she sees, so step lightly and watch your behinds! She'll get you right in the tush if you're not careful."

Shortly after Ralph finished telling them about Mocha, he left them to go back to the tree and see what his kids were doing. He and Batty went to go nap by the fence where they could see the house and the truck that was still parked outside. He thought about what Ralph had told them and about the place they were now. He knew this place was different than "The Before." He had heard of sanctuaries from the raccoon family and some of the other farm animals at the different places they had been, and the stories were mostly good. They were usually run by loving people trying to give the residents forever homes and safe environments. Of course, there were the stories of the ones that took in too many to care for and had to be rescued by the other ones, and the families that had been built were split up, but he didn't hear too many of those. It didn't sound like Kayleigh's sanctuary was a bad one, and now Mocha had a new home. He realized he had been feeling more and more hopeful as each day passed. This was a nice thought as he drifted off to sleep.

"Heyheyheyheyheyheyhey! Wake up!" Batty's voice was booming in his ear.

He rolled over and whipped his head back and forth as he took in his surroundings and looked for the danger. Batty was hopping on one foot and turning in circles. He still couldn't see what the issue was.

"What is it?" he asked frantically.

Batty yelled at the top of his lungs, "She hit me in the butt! She hit me in the butt!" He stuck out his bottom lip as he pouted and went to plop into a mudhole. Water splashed out the sides as he sank his hindquarters into the cool mud with a look of relief on his face.

He saw something whiz by him, and he quickly turned around. Mocha was running full speed down the pasture toward the big tree! She was cackling and jumping as she barreled toward the other side of the pasture. He could hear her "Aieeeeeeee hahhahahhhahha!" all the way there.

His heart had finally slowed down, and he spent a moment taking it all in. He saw Batty moving his tush back and forth in the mud and Mocha now happily munching on pine needles underneath the tree. Nelson was over at one of the troughs practicing his backstroke and sunning his belly. The big white truck was gone, and the house was quiet. All he saw was peace.

Batty plopped over in the mud with a big splash, bringing him back to what was happening around him. Batty told him he had been napping when Mocha came out of nowhere and headbutted him right in the behind. They both looked over at Mocha. She was munching and pretending not to look at them, but they could see her peeking sideways. She must have been put in the pasture while they were napping, but they hadn't heard a thing. Batty stood up and came out of the wallow.

He wondered if they should to go her or if she would come to them. For now, she was pretending to ignore them while still looking at them out of the corner of her eye. He nudged Batty, and they started walking toward her. She turned and faced them, dropped the pine cone that was in her mouth, and ran full speed toward Batty. "Aieeeeeeeeeeeeee!"

Batty's eyes widened, and he stepped back when he realized she wasn't slowing. He turned around, and his little legs started moving toward the barn, but it was too late. She was already to them by that time. *Oooooof!* She headbutted him in his right butt cheek and got a big grin on her face as she hopped sideways and away from them. When she had enough distance between them, she slowed to a walk and continued toward the barn with her chin up, as if she were balancing a crown on her head. She looked almost regal as she went into Batty's stall, lay down, and promptly fell asleep.

"Well, I guess Ralph was right to say don't turn my back!" declared Batty.

"Yup, let's give her tonight and see how she is tomorrow."

He and Batty turned back to the comfy hill they had been napping on and decided they would spend the night under the stars. After all, it was beautiful out, and the nights they were still outside at dinnertime CJ would bring food to them and let them eat in the fresh air. That night, they had a nice dinner outside and slept in the cool air under the stars.

In the morning, they awoke early, eager to see what the day brought with their new barn mate. He and Batty walked quietly to the barn and saw Mocha asleep in

Batty's stall with her head and legs tucked in tight. They slowly entered the barn and stood in front of the opening. She didn't stir as they watched her sleep. Batty said she looked peaceful and not at all like the manic hellion who had attacked him yesterday.

He let out a laugh in response to Batty's musings. Mocha opened one eye, saw them standing there, and immediately jumped to her feet and backed up into the corner of the stall. She put her head down, pointed her horns toward them, and looked ready to charge.

He said, "Hey! We're just here to say hi and introduce ourselves. We don't want to scare you."

She lifted her head and looked sideways at them. He gave her their names and told her the story of how they came to be there and where they had come from. He could see her start to relax as he talked. He saw she was listening, and he continued to talk to put her at ease. He even got in some stories about the raccoons. He was happy to see that got a shy smile out of her. He finished his story and asked her if they could give her a tour of the place. He didn't want to ask her too much or push her to talk about her past. He knew from his own experience that it would come out when she felt safe and was ready to talk.

Mocha said she would like a tour, and they all three walked out of the barn. He started with the side pasture where the sun shades had been put up the previous week. He showed her them and told her all about the giant and the skinny one and how kind they had been when they were building the barn. He showed her where they poured concrete for the holes for the shades and talked about how they went up over some of the mudholes. He pointed out Nelson's favorite mudhole, but they didn't see him anywhere, so he said he would introduce them next time the little frog was around.

Batty then took over the tour and went pasture to pasture, pointing out all the best nap spots, where to take in sun in the morning, and where the woman brought treats every afternoon and left them if they were napping. He noticed that Batty was very excited to show off the area, and he realized this was probably the first time his brother had any area to share. Batty talked nonstop for an hour as they went all around the property, and Mocha became chattier, asking questions about their time there and what they liked best. He chuckled to himself as he noticed that Batty was careful not to turn his backside toward her at any time.

CJ came out of the house and walked over to the barn to feed them breakfast, and they thought that was a perfect way to finish up the tour. They were at the giant pine at this time and walked back to the barn to eat, finding some fresh strawberries in their bowls. Mocha looked much more relaxed than she had before the tour, and she munched happily as they ate. She said that the previous night in Batty's stall, she had been visited by Jacob, the bull snake who had recently moved into the barn and that he had brought her some of the peanuts he had been hoarding behind the boards as a welcome gift. She finished eating and said she thought she would go thank him since she had pretended to be asleep when he came into the stall. She hopped behind the barn to go look for him. He and Batty thought this was a fine time for a nap. They took themselves over to one of the shaded mudholes and sank right in to enjoy the late morning sun.

The spring seemed to fly by, and the summer came on quickly. He spent the days grateful for the barn they now lived in. He remembered how hard it had been to live outside with no shelter and the heat on his dry skin that had made it crack. Now there were fans that sprayed a cool mist of water on them during the heat of the day and plenty of cool mudholes to relax in, and every few days, there were volunteers who came out to do some of the chores around the sanctuary. He got to meet a lot of people, and Batty loved the extra treats they would bring. Batty and Mocha would run up to the fences near where the people would gather around the trailer to take breaks and eat. They would compete to see who could look cuter and get more treats. Mocha would bat her eyes while tilting her head at the volunteers and she usually won.

The treats were nice, but his favorite day was Sunday. He waited every week for Sunday to come around. His favorite person was a woman named Aurora. She would come out and talk to him while giving him special treats from her garden. He followed her around while she fluffed and changed straw in the stalls and told him of her week outside the sanctuary. She talked about her family and her important work but mostly about how she had waited all week to come see him. He had grown to trust her and her kind smile. At the end of every visit, she would put away all her tools and sit down on the ground in front of him to scratch behind his ears. She would tell him how much she loved him and how important he was. It made him feel warm inside, and the kindness reminded him of the little girl he once knew. Last Sunday, she gave him a kiss right on his snout!

He found himself thinking less and less of "The Before." He knew Batty was also forgetting the past, as he didn't have to wake him from his nightmares like he used to. He thought it might have been spring when Batty had last cried out in his sleep. Mocha was settling in as well.

She had taken a stall right next to Batty's. During the cooler nights, she would go sit in Batty's stall, and they would talk until they both fell asleep in the straw. On the hot nights, he and Batty would sleep under the stars, and the last two nights Mocha had joined them. He showed them both the constellations he had been taught by the little girl, and all three played a game of who could spot the Little Dipper the fastest. The winner got the first pick of the mudholes in the morning, and that was always a nice way to start the day.

The days went on like this until the weather turned cooler and they were spending more nights in their stalls. One morning, they awoke to the sound of Jack and the kids up out at the house. They wandered over to the fence by the hill and tried to hear what the humans were talking about. It couldn't be about their hooves, as Jack had been out the previous week to trim both theirs and Mocha's hooves, and they looked spectacular. He turned his ears toward the house in an attempt to hear better when a very long horse trailer pulled into the front gate. He and Batty looked at each other and shrugged. He had no idea what was happening now, but it was exciting, and he couldn't help but feel a little of the old nervousness in his belly. It had been a long time since he thought of the other places, especially "The Before," and he didn't want to think of being moved again.

He told his brother they should go get Mocha from out in the back pasture, where she was munching on the last of the summer flowers. He made himself sound very excited, and his mood was catching. Batty looked at him delightedly and ran behind the barn to get her.

He watched the trailer come in and back up to the shed they had originally been in. Mocha and Batty came running up just as the door of the trailer opened, and they watched as someone walked out of the trailer and into the shed. They thought they saw a flash of black and white, but their view was now blocked by Jack, the kids, and the two cowboys who had come out of the truck. By the time the people all moved away from the trailer, they couldn't see anyone.

They sat out by the hill all morning and into the afternoon, until the trailer was gone, Jack and the kids left, and CJ went back into the house. They hadn't seen any movement from the shed and had not heard a peep. They moved back to the barn, where they could see the entrance to the shed through the trees, but nothing was happening. They watched until after dinner and finally went to bed. He wondered if they had seen anyone go in there at all.

The next morning, he had forgotten about the excitement and stayed in bed longer than usual. It was cool and cloudy out and perfect weather for sleeping in. He heard CJ coming with breakfast and slowly shook off the warm straw while Batty and Mocha got up from the stall next to him. They all three went out to the feeding area and drank some cool water as CJ cut up some fresh pumpkin to add to their bowls. Of all the new foods they were being fed, pumpkin was his favorite so far, and on the weekends, when the volunteers came out, they would bring them as treats and give him an entire one all to himself. He liked taking his pumpkin out underneath the big pine and munching away on the sweet meat as he shared it with Ralph and his family. Occasionally, the barn cats would come out and roll around in the pine needles as they talked, and it felt like a family brunch.

CJ fed them and continued cutting up pumpkins for two additional bowls. He wondered if they were going to get an extra helping today, like they did when it was cold out last winter. Then he suddenly remembered the trailer. He perked up and looked over at the shed, but it was still quiet with no sign of anyone inside. She was telling them about the week and the new greenhouse going in so next year they would have fresh produce all year round.

He was still looking at the shed when he heard her say something about a pony. A pony? Was there a new horse over there? He hadn't been paying attention to her words while he was eating, so he struggled to make sense of what she was saying. Now he heard the word *soda*. She was having a soda? She got a soda? His brain knew there was something to what she was saying, and it was slowly coming together. Wait. *Pony* and *Soda*? Pony Boy and Soda Pop. He hadn't heard those names in a very long time. He couldn't breathe. He was suddenly filled with immense hope and heartache at the same time.

He looked over at the shed. He was very attuned to what she was saying now. She said that they had two new residents who came in yesterday, and their names were Pony Boy and Soda Pop. She was going to go feed them now, and in two weeks, the newcomers would be joining them in the barn. But for the time being, they were in quarantine to make sure their health was good, as they had come from Kayleigh's place where they had been re-covering after their rescue a few months ago.

He awoke with three worried faces staring down at him. CJ, Batty, and Mocha were all in a circle standing over him, watching as he got to his feet.

The woman said, "Oh my gosh, are you okay, handsome? You just passed out. What happened? Is it too hot in here, or should I call Jack?" She reached down and felt his face as she kissed his head.

He shook off the terror as it faded to the back of his mind while he tried to make sense of Pony and Soda being here. In this place. After he'd thought he'd lost his friends to the men that took pigs away to the large barn to be loaded into trucks. He knew no one ever came back from there.

As his heart rate slowed down, his memory came back, and he relived the trauma. He, Batty, Pony Boy, and Soda Pop had been fast friends for a time in the very bad place they called "The Before." Soda and Pony were a little older and had been there for a long time. They had taught him and Batty how to go to places in their minds when the fear got to be too much. They explained they called the place with all the barns and farrowing crates "The Before" because there were good places they knew of in the world, where humans were nice and treats were plentiful, where they could nap in the sun and feel the ground beneath their feet. They talked of the trees he had heard about and cool rain showers that brought rainbows. They taught them there was a place called "The After," and they just needed to survive "The Before." When they got scared or heard the other pigs' cries across the pastures, they could escape in their minds into a fantasy world where all was right and they were safe.

Pony and Soda had escaped being taken in the trucks so far because they were unlike the other ones that were usually taken away. Pony was smaller than the rest of the pigs on the factory farm. He had been the runt of his litter, and his leg had never grown out properly. Soda was from two different types of parents and not the kind they could make put on weight quickly by overfeeding. This meant both Pony and Soda were largely left alone in the big operation, and one day they were moved to the back of the property into a decrepit barn, as they wouldn't be worth as much as larger pigs when sold for meat.

On the day he and Batty lost their friends, four big men showed up from across the pasture. As they heard the men approach, Pony and Soda had them all huddle in the corner and make themselves as small as possible. He shut his eyes tight and told Batty to go to the secret place in his mind where he felt warm and safe and block out all the talking now. He kept his ears open so he could keep Batty safe.

He could hear the men talking at the door as they looked at the four of them. The largest one turned to the one holding a pitchfork and asked which ones they were to take. The man responded, "Doesn't matter. We were told to get two of them since there is room on this truck that's going to the processing plant this morning. Driver doesn't want to go light, so grab the ones that don't fight as much."

Terror overtook him, and he looked at Pony and Soda. They were gazing at each other with almost calm expressions on their faces. Soda nodded and stepped forward while Pony put his entire body in front of him and Batty. The men rushed forward, grabbed Soda, and dragged him toward the door. He watched, frozen. He cried out for Soda to fight. Pony stepped toward the men, and they grabbed him next. Pony couldn't get his smaller leg moving fast enough, and two of them pulled him out the door by his little arms and started dragging his body across the field.

Soda looked at him calmly and told him it was okay; he needed to hang in there and protect his brother. He said he and Pony had been there long enough, and it was their jobs now to give them more time to get to "The After." Soda told him not to lose hope. There were still beautiful things to see in the world, and he had hope that they would get to see them all. Then Soda let himself be dragged off.

He watched, horrified, as they all moved across the field. As they walked, the one with the pitchfork poked at their skin and laughed each time it drew blood. One of the other men took a can of spray paint out of his pocket and sprayed numbers on both of them. The paint mixed with the blood running down their bodies as they approached the big barn. He could see tears streaming down their faces, but both looked calm. Soda was telling Pony he loved him very much, and he was so happy to have spent his life with him. That was the last he heard. He couldn't take the horror and went to the place in his mind where he was free from danger. He and Batty spent the night there, huddled in the corner, both in the secret places in their minds. The boys had saved him and his brother one last time. They had saved him, and it was always their cries he heard when he thought about "The Before."

His mind came back to the present. Could they really be here? The guilt he felt for surviving "The Before" mixed with hope that Pony and Soda could be over in the little shed, and he felt nauseous. He looked up.

CJ was still looking at him worriedly. He tried on his best smile and stood up to get a drink of water to calm his stomach. She said she would check in on him in a bit. She took the two bowls out of the barn and went in the direction of the shed.

Batty said quietly, "Could it really be them?"

He said he didn't know and looked across at the shed. They saw the woman go into the shed with the bowls, talking to someone in there. They still could not see anyone, and they stayed there, focused on the door, for the next few hours. No one came out.

He finally had to look away. His mind continued to race with all the what-ifs, wondering how it could possibly be Pony and Soda. He'd seen them taken. How could they be there now? It must be someone else. He went to his stall alone, leaving Batty and Mocha to talk quietly. Batty was slowly telling Mocha about "The Before." She was crying as he told her the story, and he couldn't watch, as the survivor's guilt overtook him. He lay down, and his mind wandered to what had happened next.

He and Batty had spent the next few months in "The Before" being hypervigilant. They would sleep in turns while the other kept watch. They were aware they were being overfed and fattened up, but no one came to get them, and they spent the time stressed and tired, ever watchful for the men with the sharp tools and spray can. They weren't sure why they were still there. They knew the humans remembered them in the back barn, or they wouldn't be getting thrown food. He and Batty finally stopped asking one another questions, as there were no answers.

One day, some men they hadn't seen before showed up at the back fence, and they could hear them talking about the barn. They had been sent to see what needed to be done to tear it down, as it had no water lines or electricity and the roof was falling in. One asked where the animals inside would go, as he gestured to their corner. Another answered that he thought they would be moved to the big barn next week before the structure came down. Terror struck his heart again. He was too exhausted to move. The stress of keeping an eye out for what was coming next was too much. He looked at Batty and saw the fear. He couldn't reassure him, and they both just sat there and felt the last of the hope drain away. Pony and Soda had sacrificed themselves for nothing. They would not make it to "The After."

That night, as he and Batty huddled together and drifted in and out of tortured sleep, he heard whispers. There were people at the fence talking quietly. He thought it strange that they would come in the night for them, but he shut his eyes and went to his safe place.

He suddenly felt a light touch on his arm. His eyes flew open. He saw a woman with kind eyes and a soft voice bending over him, whispering to him. "Hey boy, let's get you out of here. Will you come with us?"

His mind couldn't reconcile what he was expecting when they got him with what was happening now. He just stared.

"Please get up. Please come with us. We are here to rescue some piglets from the ferrying crates, and we saw you two back here. We have room. Please come."

He didn't see any of the hate on her face that he had seen on the men's, and he didn't see any pitchfork. He stood up slowly and nudged Batty to get up, and they followed the woman.

They were directed behind the falling-down barn to a hole that had been cut in the fence and a trailer parked on the other side. They went up the ramp, trying to stay alert to possible danger but too exhausted to make sense of it all. They weren't being hurt, and that was all that mattered in the moment. He had Batty go to the corner, he lay down in front of him, and the doors closed. He retreated back into his mind and blacked out everything else around him.

He felt the light touch again. He opened his eyes and saw the trailer had stopped. The same kind woman was talking to him, saying he was at a rescue in Texas. It wasn't the best, and there were too many animals, but she knew at least he would be safe from slaughter while they looked for a better place for him. He didn't have the strength to do anything but go where directed and make sure Batty was next to him. All he cared about was that they were together. They were sent to a small pile of hay in a corner of the yard with some pellets on the ground. They slumped down into the hay and back into their minds as they heard the trailer drive away.

He and Batty were there for what felt like years, although looking back, it was probably only a few months. There were many, many animals in the place they had been brought to, and they all shared a limited amount of food. There were goats, small pigs unlike themselves, chickens, and a cow, although the cow was taken around the back one day by the cruel man and never came back. They learned to stay far away from the man when he was out in the yard. He was quick to lash out with kicks if he saw someone within reach. Batty thought he was deliberately not feeding anyone enough, but it was all they could do to simply survive the horrors of what they had been through; they could not worry about what was happening to the rest of the animals there. They were in survival mode and got through the days by escaping as Pony and Soda had taught them. He thought of them often, and most nights, he cried himself to sleep, careful to not let Batty see.

One afternoon when the woman who ran the place was out, the man drove an old rusted trailer up to the fence and told them both to get in, as they were too big and taking up too much room, eating him out of house and home. They quickly got in before the kicks could come. He drove the trailer very fast. The man did not slow down around the curves, and they found themselves being cut by the sharp edges that had rusted out with the age and weather. As they were being moved, what was left of the roof flew off and bounced down the road. Suddenly, the trailer stopped, and they were slammed into the front. The man got out, ran to the back, and unhooked the trailer from the truck. He opened the rusty door, gave one last look at them, and he was gone.

He looked out the door and across the field, where he saw a house and an old woman looking out the window at them. He and Batty huddled together, tired and unsure, but grateful not to see a large barn.

His thoughts came back to the present and whoever might be in the shed. He got up from his stall and went outside. He was ready to see who was inside. He knew for certain in his heart he was safe here. He had been shown nothing but love and safety and had not gone to the place in his mind since those first few weeks when they arrived. He knew the trauma they had endured was over.

He stood up tall and walked over to the side pasture closest to the shed. He looked at the door, straining to see inside. He didn't see movement, but he heard voices. He gathered up his hope and courage. He cleared his throat. "Hmmmmppph, ack, hmmffft." No reaction from inside.

He tried again. "Hmmmmfffft!" Nothing. He summoned all his bravery and yelled, "Hey, you there! Come out!"

He waited. He heard stirring. He saw a face poke out of the door. It was Soda Pop, his old friend and mentor and the one he'd thought he had lost! Another face came out. Pony Boy! They did not see him at first, as the sun was in their eyes. It took a few seconds to adjust, and then their eyes went wide. They both started shouting at once and ran over to the fence. This got Batty's and Mocha's attention, and they raced over to him.

All four pigs were now bawling and talking and crying. No one could hear what the others were saying, but happy grins and streaming tears were on all faces. Soda Pop stood on his hind legs and did a dance as Pony Boy couldn't contain his joy any longer and started doing zoomies across the small quarantine pasture. Back and forth, back and forth. Batty joined him from his fence line.

Ralph, having heard the commotion, flew down and perched on the roof of the shed, watching. Nelson hopped out of one of the mudholes, concerned he was going to get run over, and hopped away to the tree, keeping an eye on them all. Now the guardian dogs had run over to the fence to see what the ruckus was about and make sure the new intakes were safe. They watched and took in the reunion with big grins on their faces and, confident all was good, went back to patrolling the outer fence line. This reunion celebration among old friends went on for a full ten minutes until they had burned off the energy and all four just sat down on their butts with huge smiles on their faces, fully present in the joy of being alive and seeing each other.

The quarantine shed Pony and Soda were in and the pasture he and Batty were in had a good eight feet run between the two areas. They all settled down behind their respective fences, and after the initial hellos and exclamations of astonishment were over, Pony and Soda told him and Batty what had happened to them after they were taken away to the barn.

They had been put in the barn, in a queue, and loaded into the truck that was waiting. They were on the top level of the truck next to each other and had an oval window that let in air as it was driven, although it was too hot and crowded to move. They were driven down the highway and up through the mountains. They had been on the trip for about thirty minutes when they heard a screeching from the truck's brakes and it went spinning. They thought they spun around four or five times before the cab fell over on its side and broke away from the trailer. This caused an opening in the metal side of the trailer and the four levels with pigs on them to collapse in on each other. Because Pony and Soda were on the top level and near the opening, they were able to scramble out and away from the wreckage.

Most of the pigs had not survived the crash, and as they quickly took in their surroundings, Pony and Soda yelled for those who were alive and could walk to follow them. They ran down the ravine and into the woods. There were fourteen who survived that first night, and each day they moved a little farther into the woods and away from people. They foraged during the day and had cool streams to drink from. They spent the next year as a herd, moving at night, sleeping in the day, and staying away from all human contact. No one seemed to be looking for them, and they enjoyed the freedom and movement in nature, although it was rough at times scavenging, they were all losing some muscle and weight, and there were many predators. They lost five of their herd to coyotes, three to sickness, and two from their initial injuries from the wreck. They were down to just four, and Pony and Soda decided it was time to find some help, as Burt, the largest of them, was not doing well. He had been bred so large that his little legs could not support his large frame, and he was slowing down. Each night, he was a bit slower, and they were concerned that with winter coming, he would be taken by wolves. They had seen a pack following them the last few nights and knew it was only a matter of time.

The next week, they were flanked and attacked. Burt survived, fighting them off with his sharp tusks, but he was injured and needed immediate help. The next day, Soda left Pony with Burt and his brother and traveled down the mountain to the nearest farm to check it out. He did not know this at the time, but they had traveled over three hundred miles that year and were in Santa Fe above Kayleigh's place. She was looking out the kitchen window and saw him come out of the woods. She knew instinctively he had someone in trouble and followed him up the mountain to Burt and the others. She brought in help and took the four of them in, and they had spent the winter at her place recuperating from the loss of weight and rigors of living outside. Then she and Jack had worked out a plan for them to be brought to CJ's place. Burt and his brother had stayed with Kayleigh, and he and Pony were transferred to what they were told was a new sanctuary down near Edgewood.

Soda looked at him and Batty as the story ended. He wondered if Soda could tell how guilty and ashamed he felt that he and his brother had escaped the brutal ordeal their old friends had endured. Could Soda tell he was thinking about the last time they saw each other?

Smiling gently, Soda gestured around at the pastures, the wide-open spaces, the mudholes, the wonderfully large barn, and the giant tree behind him. "You protected your brother and survived. Now, you are witnessing the beauty around you, just as I hoped. Life often differs from our expectations, but the future holds endless possibilities. This is what happens when you don't give up. This is what happens when you stay alive. This, my beautiful friend, is your 'After,' and you made it." Soda smiled as he looked up at the giant tree. "I can't wait to see what the future holds."

Suddenly, Ralph swooped down. "Hey, kids! Jack's pulling a horse trailer down the road on his way here. Looks like we have some new guests. Let's all welcome them, shall we?" Ralph turned and looked at him. "Hemmers, my friend, why don't you lead the way."

Hemmingway stepped forward, filled with immense joy, ready to see what came next.

The Ponderosa

The Mighty Ponderosa

The
Beginning

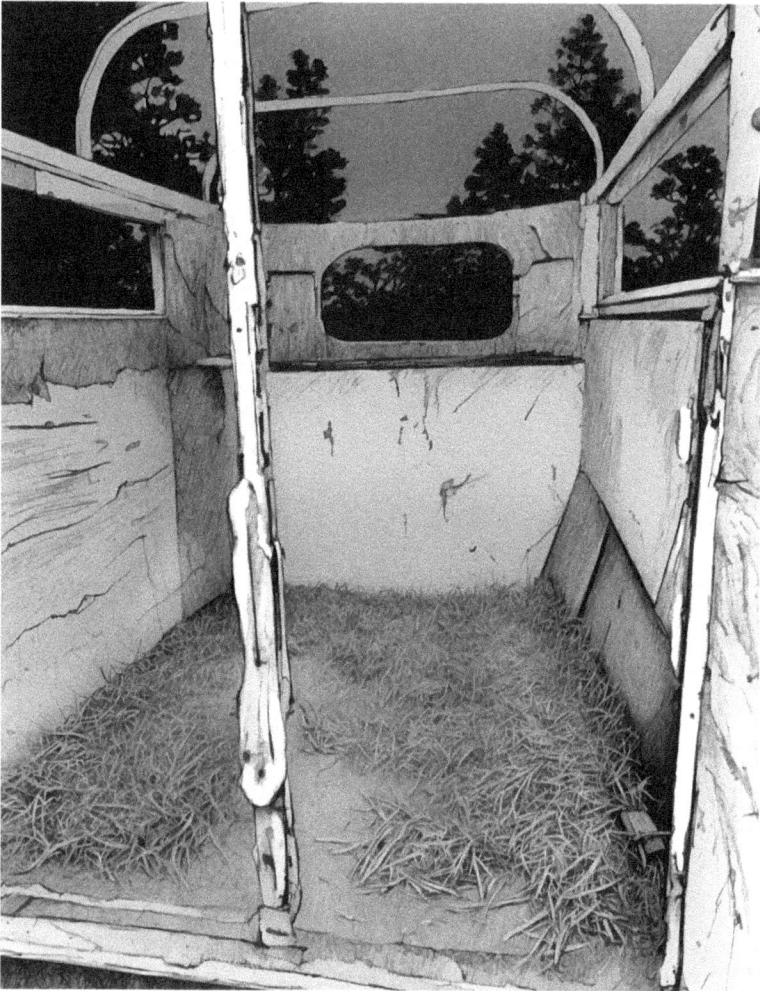

The following are photos of the actual trailer Hemmingway and Batty were brought to the sanctuary in and had been living in for more than a year, along with a photo of each of them their first day.

The Beginning

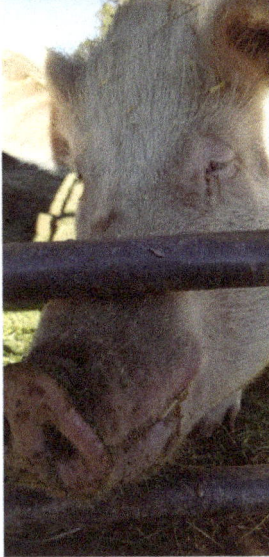

Their
After

Consider that animals, like us, have one life. It is their life, their only life, and as important to them as our own life is to us.

—Jill Robinson

Their beautiful, valuable, joyful After.

Hemmingway

My hope is that we learn from the animals what it is we need to become better people.

—Colleen Patrick-Goudreau

Hemmers

Batty

Really, my message is simple. It's a message of compassion. In this world that is spinning madly out of control, we have to realize that we're all related. We have to try to live harmoniously.

—Woody Harrelson

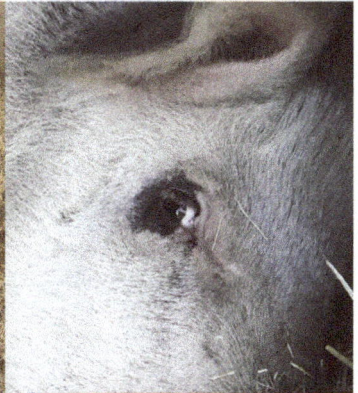

Soda Pop

Most people I've met who weren't kind to animals weren't kind to people either. Kindness is kindness. Simple as that.

—Ricky Gervais

Soda Pop

Pony Boy

There is no fundamental difference between man and animals in their ability to feel pleasure and pain, happiness, and misery.

—Charles Darwin

Mocha

The soul is the same in all living creatures, although the body of each is different.

—Hippocrates

Mocha

Around
the
Sanctuary

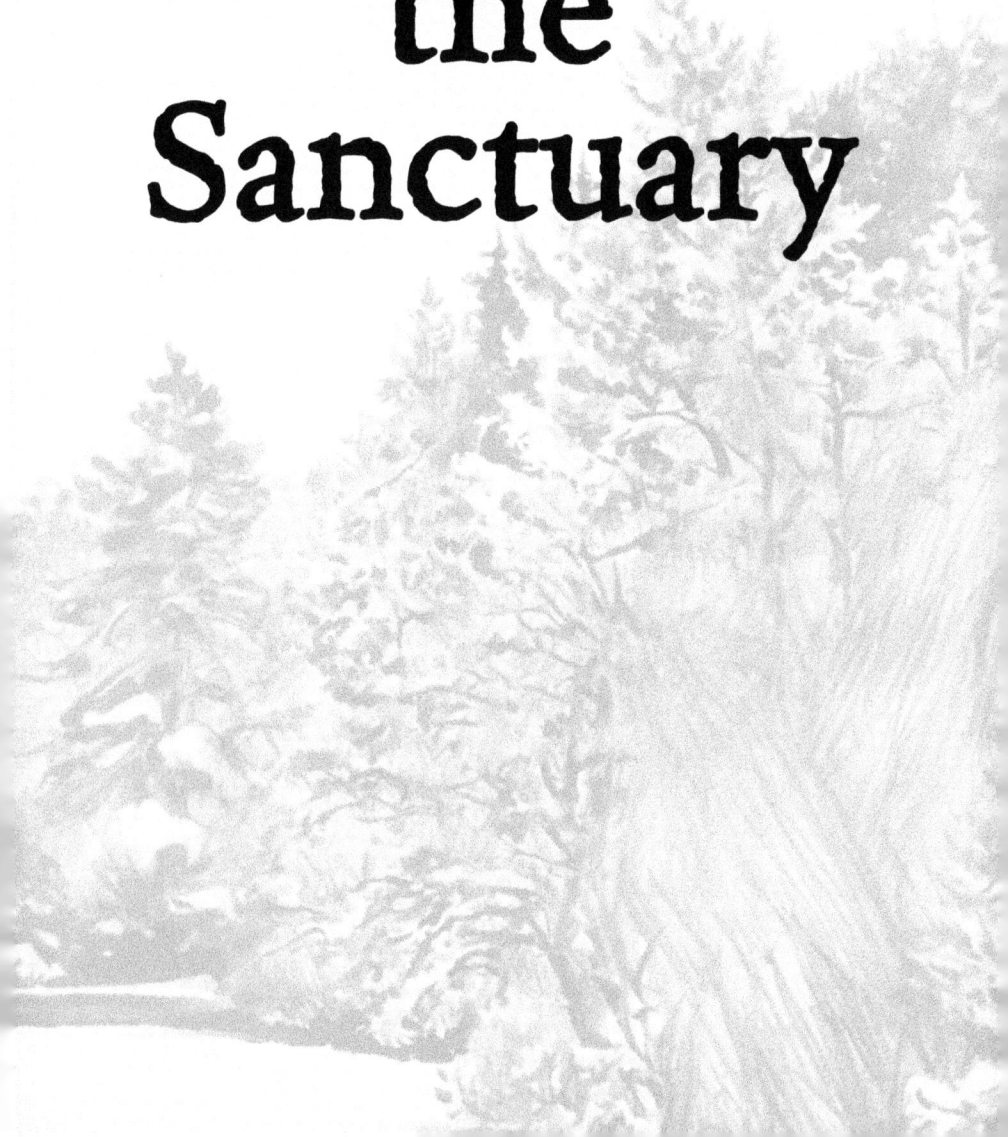

The idea that some lives matter less is the root of all that is wrong in the world.

—Dr. Paul Farmer

Julie and Gaby with Pony Boy

The following photos capture residents and everyday life around the sanctuary. Despite being one of the most challenging and heart-wrenching endeavors of our lives, it is our privilege not only to get to know the animals individually but also to ensure their lifelong safety. It has truly been an honor. To the rescuers who work tirelessly with these individuals every day, we are in awe of your strength and capacity for relentless love and loss. Your dedication makes a profound difference in each of their lives. Stay in the fight.

The following quotation by Joaquin Phoenix is one that eloquently expresses the beliefs of staff and volunteers who work at the sanctuary:

> I think whether we're talking about gender inequality or racism or queer rights or indigenous rights or animal rights, we're talking about the fight against injustice. We're talking about the fight against the belief that one nation, one people, one race, one gender, or one species has the right to dominate, control, and use and exploit another with impunity. I think that we've become very disconnected from the natural world. And many of us, what we're guilty of, is an egocentric worldview, the belief that we're the center of the universe. We go into the natural world and we plunder it for its resources. We feel entitled to artificially inseminate a cow, and when she gives birth, we steal her baby, even though her cries of anguish are unmistakable. And then we take her

milk that's intended for her calf and we put it in our coffee and our cereal, and I think we fear the idea of personal change, because we think that we have to sacrifice something, to give something up. But human beings, at our best, are so inventive and creative and ingenious, and I think that when we use love and compassion as our guiding principles, we can create, develop, and implement systems of change that are beneficial to all sentient beings and to the environment.

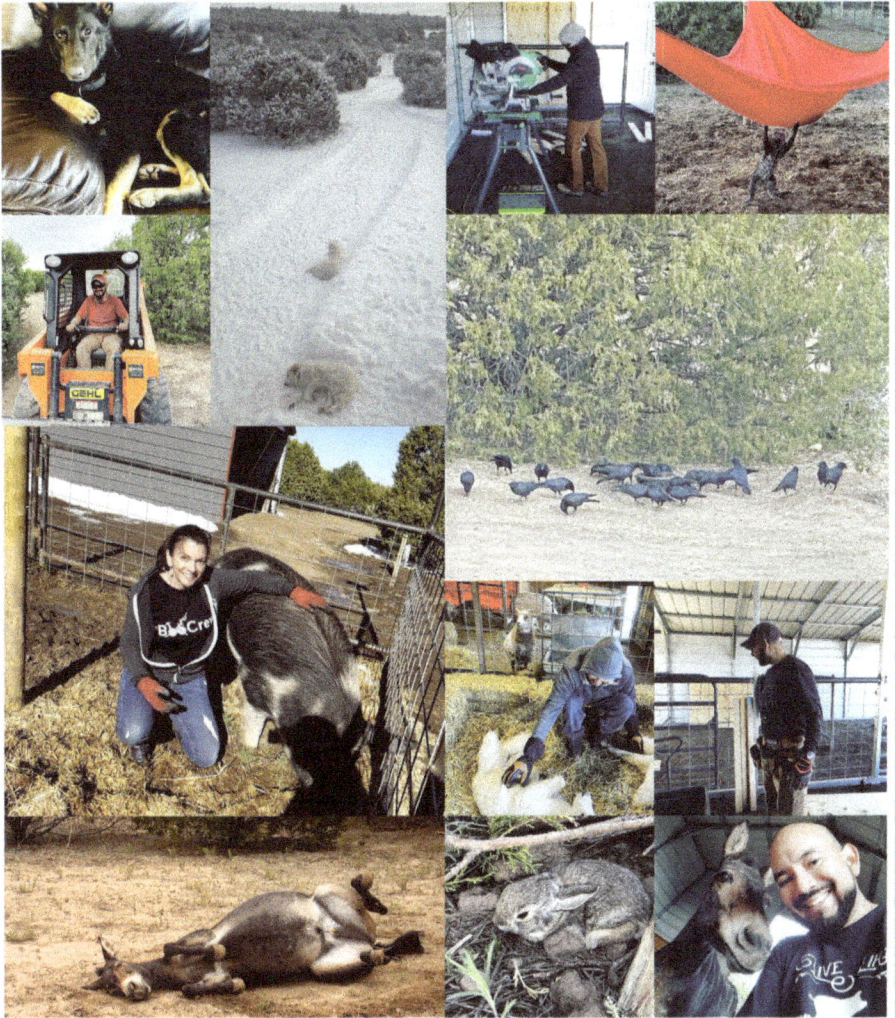

Around the Sanctuary

155

Around the Sanctuary

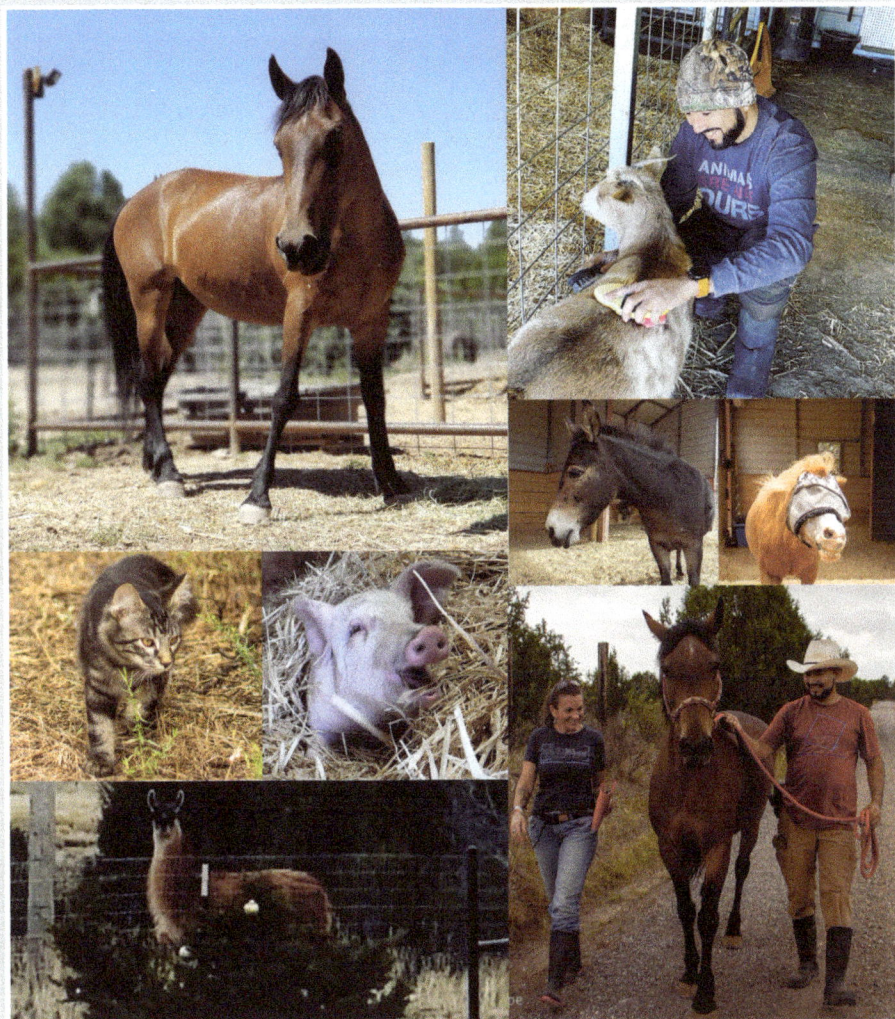

Around the Sanctuary

Around the Sanctuary

Around the Sanctuary

Around the Sanctuary

Around the Sanctuary

Around the Sanctuary

Around the Sanctuary

Around the Sanctuary

Around the Sanctuary

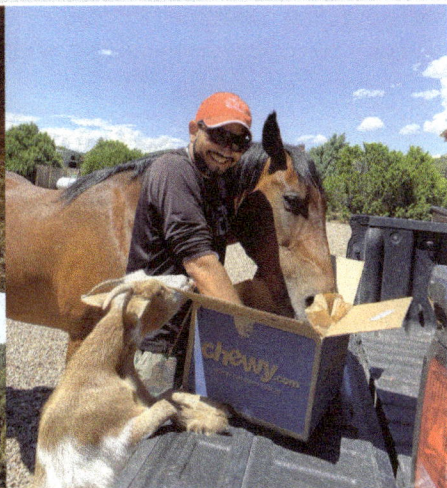

Around the Sanctuary

Around the Sanctuary

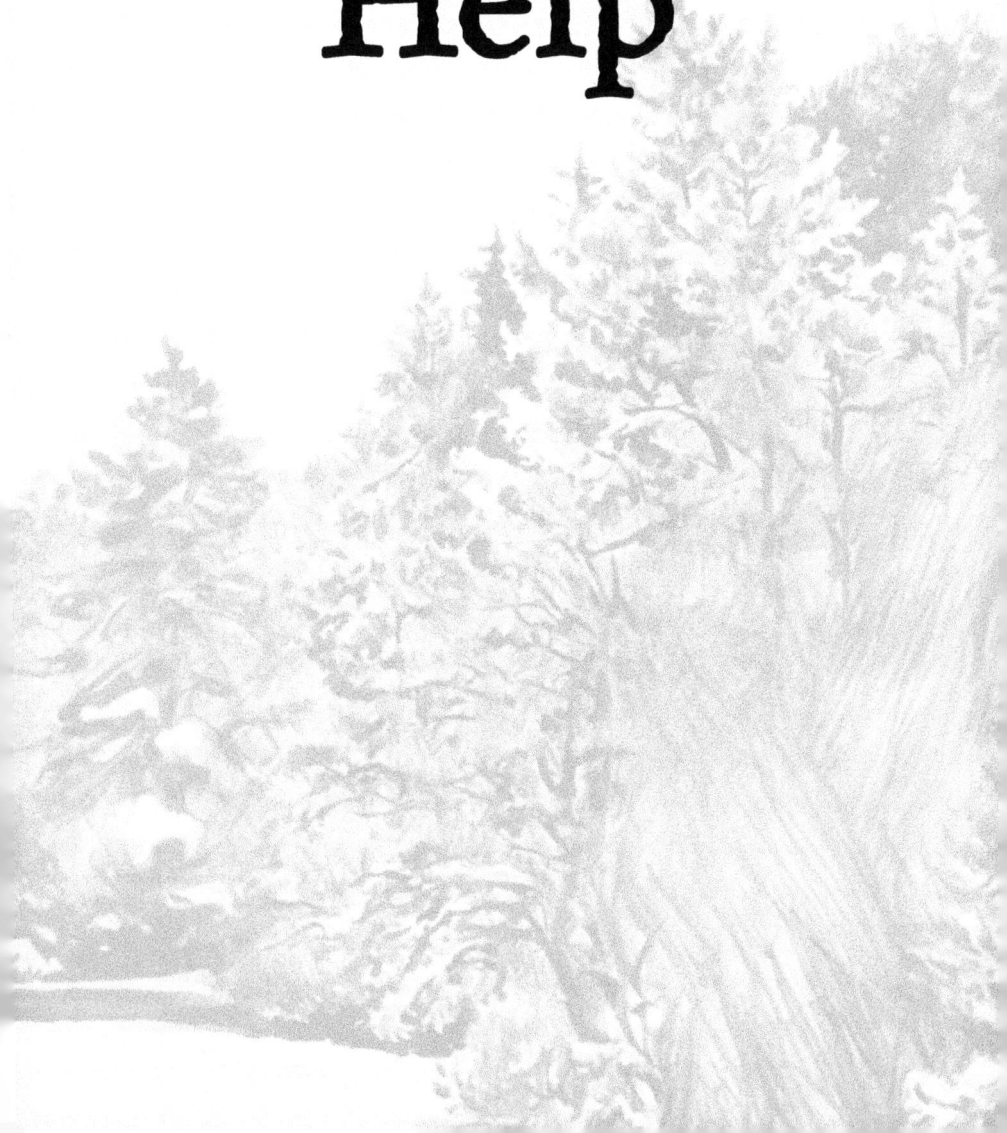

How to Help

With deep gratitude, proceeds from The After are donated through the North America Farm Sanctuary Coalition LLC to support the Misfits of Oz Farm Sanctuary, a 501(c)3 nonprofit organization.

Shanda's unwavering advocacy for animals and dedication to providing safe havens for all ensure that Hemmingway, his family, and all the Misfits are fiercely loved and will receive the best care for the rest of their lives.

Please visit us to find out more at:
www.nafarmsanctuarycoalition.org

NORTH · AMERICA
Farm Sanctuary
Coalition

EDUCATION . CONSERVATION . ADVOCACY

A Note from the Founder of Misfits of Oz:

When I started Misfits of Oz Farm Sanctuary back in 2018, I wanted to create a space so magical that the animals who joined us would forget about the abuse and neglect many of them had suffered in their pasts. Over the years, we have taken in animals from such a variety of cases—some from starvation by people believing in the "micro pig" myth; some from animal control seizures; some from factory farms, animals with special needs, or in hospice care; and some from amazing humans who loved them but needed to make a change to better the lives of the animals.

Misfits of Oz has been a dream to build and run. As a current home to fifty-five animals and growing, we get the opportunity to provide a magical life to those in our care. We get to show unconditional love; proper diet, veterinary care, and hoof and tusk care; socialization; and a sense of safety and family. This dream is only possible because of incredible humans who support our mission and believe in our future—the people who love the animals and support their growth and happiness. It's these humans who make this life happen by donating, sponsoring, volunteering, and joining our social media to help us spread our message of animal care, compassion, and a vegan lifestyle.

Our mission is to create a better world for farmed animals by showing their unique personalities, emotional bandwidth, and true intelligence. My world has been forever changed by the love and appreciation I feel from these animals every day. We hope you will join the Misfits movement to create a better planet for the animals, who are so deserving.

To donate or get involved, please visit us at:
www.misfitsofoz.org

Or see us on socials at:

Instagram at
@misftsof_oz

Facebook at
Misfits of Oz Farm Sanctuary

You can make a difference by making compassionate choices. Welcome to the Misfits family, where outcasts unite.

Shanda Melendrez
Executive Director, Misfits of Oz Farm Sanctuary
PO Box 97
Edgewood, NM 87015

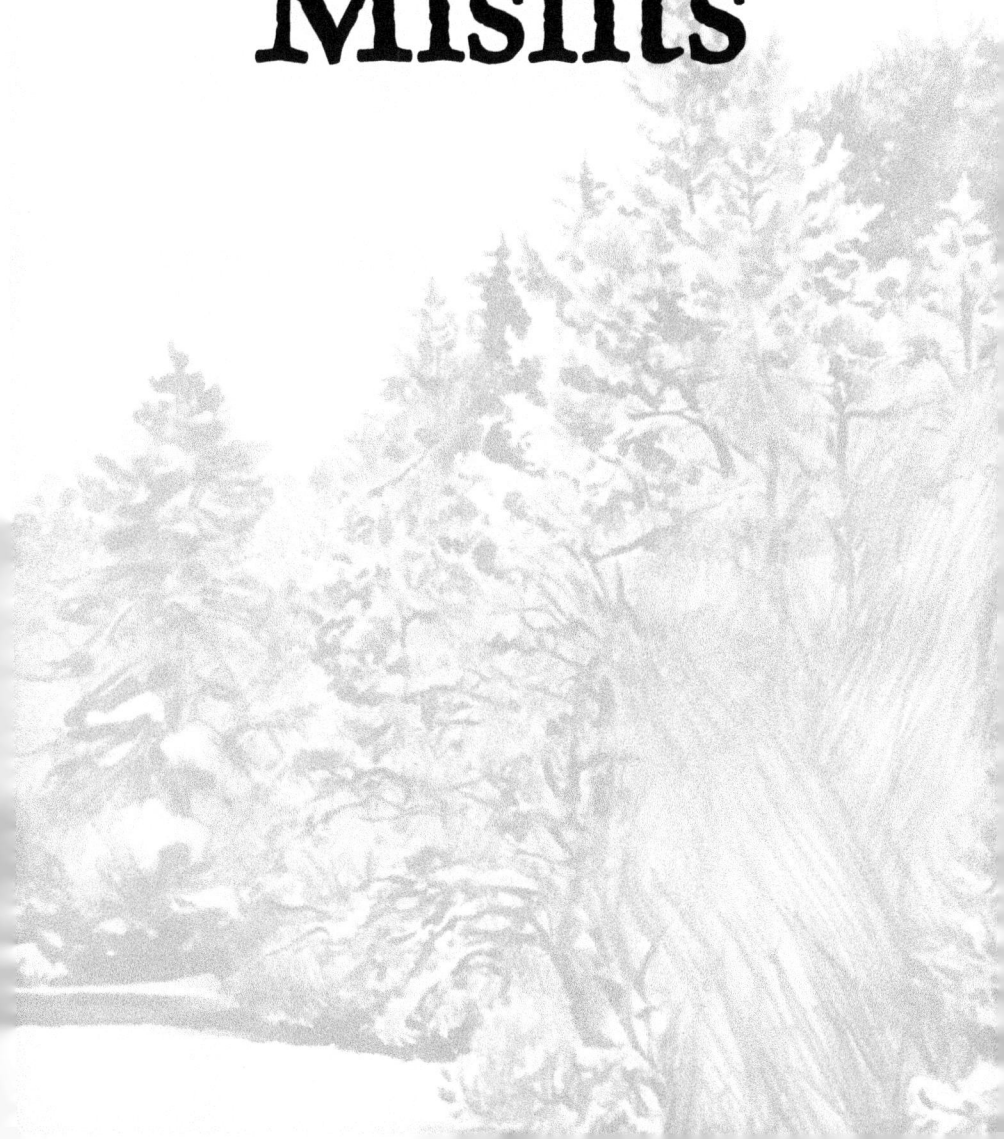

The
Misfits

It takes nothing away from a human to be kind to an animal.
—Joaquin Phoenix

Shanda and Pony Boy

The following photos are of Shanda and residents of Misfits of Oz Farm Sanctuary, where Hemmingway and his family live in their forever home.

The Misfits

The Misfits

The Misfits

The Misfits

The Misfits

The Misfits

The Misfits

The Misfits

Animals are not voiceless; you are not listening.

—Unknown

Tango and Cash

Afterword

This book has been a long time in the making and has truly been a labor of love. Both NMFS and this book owe their existence to the unwavering support of my husband, Gabriel.

Echoing the uncompromising stance of Howard Lyman, "You can't be an environmentalist and eat animal products. Period." This story honors those who courageously align their actions with their beliefs, inspiring others to reconsider their impact on our planet and all its inhabitants.

Please note that this is a work of fiction. Hemmingway did not actually write this book, nor was the author privy to the animals' conversations. **Unless otherwise indicated, all the names, characters, businesses, places, events, and incidents in this book are either the product of the author's imagination or used in a fictitious manner. Any resemblance to actual persons, living or dead, or actual events is purely coincidental.**

Hemmers

Milton Keynes UK
Ingram Content Group UK Ltd.
UKHW020646131124
450964UK00017B/109/J

9 798822 963122